Don't Call Me Names

Learning to Understand Kids with Disabilities

C.W. Graham

Illustrated by Kristy Lyons

merge
Publishing Group, LLC

ISBN 10: 0-9825699-3-9

ISBN 13: 978-0-9825699-3-1

Library of Congress Cataloging-in-Publication Data

Emerge Publishing Group, LLC
Riviera Beach, FL
www.emergepublishers.com

Acknowledgments

To my husband, Jeff.
Thank you for supporting and believing in my dreams.

To my son, Marcus, and my daughter, Jasmin.
Thanks so much for your encouragement.

Special thanks to Bettye Knighton, for your wisdom and guidance.
You have a genuine and unselfish desire to see others succeed,
and for that I am truly grateful.

To my Grandma, Elizabeth, who instilled in me my faith.
Thanks for your prayers and encouragement.

To the Just for Kids Nursing Agency (Kathi, Felisa, Aaron, Stuart, and all of
Morgann's nurses, past and present): I will never forget the day you made
it possible for Morgann to come home from the hospital, under your care,
four months old, medically fragile and with a very poor prognosis. What a
difference you have made in our lives and continue to make in the lives of so
many kids and their families. Thank you for such excellent care.

To Morgann's doctors (Dr. M. Cruz, Dr. L. Adams, Dr. T. Schechtman,
Dr. I. Stein, Dr. A. Bufo, and countless others) many thanks for your dedication
and high quality of care.

To Morgann's therapists, who always expect more.

I thank God for His confirmation and direction.

"With God all things are possible."
Matt 19:26

Dedication

This book is dedicated to my daughter, Morgann, my joy and inspiration. You continue to inspire me each and every day through your strength, courage, and determination.

To Jabari Leake and every child faced with the challenges of a disability.

"You are fearfully and wonderfully made."
Psalm 139:14

Contents

SCHOOL BUS

River Branch School

Differences
and Disabilities

Disabilities affect people in many different ways.
Some people need special nurses and some use helpful aids.
Aids are kinds of helpers to help people hear, walk, and see.
Some people have tracheostomies to help them breathe.

10

A disability can affect how a person looks, learns, or plays.
They may act or behave differently or do things in a different way.
There are some things people with disabilities can and cannot do.
That's true for all of us—we have our limits, too.

As you read through these pages, you will meet kids of all ages.
Kids with disabilities but kids just the same.
Let's hear their stories to help us better understand
the difficulties they face and their challenges, first-hand.

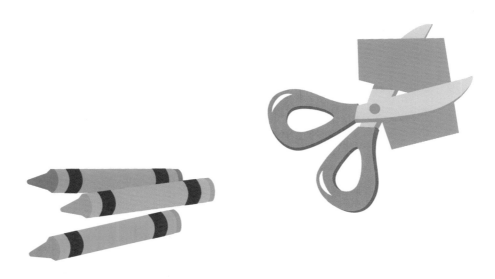

Mrs. Jane's Class

These are the students in Mrs. Jane's class.
They talk with their fingers by moving them really fast.
Some are hearing-impaired, so it's hard for them to hear.
Words are all muffled and some sounds are not clear.

Like the sound of a whistle, a friend calling their name,
the ringing of a school bell, or the falling drops of rain.
The hearing aids in their ears help them to hear.
Words are much louder and sounds are more clear.

All of Mrs. Jane's students learn to sign in the end,
to talk with one another and include everyone as friends.
What a great example practiced in this school.
Respect one another's differences is their golden rule.

Chad and Friends

Some days, Chad doesn't feel his best.
Some days he spends at home on bed rest.
His weakening muscles are a form of MD.
MD is short for muscular dystrophy.

It's harder than usual for him to walk these days.
His joints are really stiff and painful when he plays.
His friends, Todd and Andy, came over today
with a cool video to watch and a pizza on the way.

A visit from friends put a smile on Chad's face.
They shared pizza and watched *Fast Cars to the Race*.
We can all make a difference in some small way.
Be thoughtful about what you do each and every day.

Missy

This is Missy, short and cheerful as can be.
Ten-year-old Missy stands only two-foot-three.
She stands on her tiptoes to reach things up high.
Friends offer a hand when they're standing close by.

Before you start to laugh or make fun of her height,
let's hear her story to see her life just right.
Missy was born much smaller than most,
with itsy-bitsy fingers and a teeny-tiny nose.

21

22

She doesn't like it at all when people call her names.
Little people, all people, should be treated just the same.
Calling people names is not something you should do.
Always treat others, as you want them to treat you.

Some Don't Understand

Meet eight-year-old Zach; he rocks and he sways.
He lets out a squeal sometimes when he plays.
Some don't understand why he plays odd games
or why he doesn't talk much or answer to his name.

Zach has a condition: autism is its name.
Kids his age notice he doesn't act quite the same.
Some things that affect him are things you can't see.
But one thing is for sure: he's happy as can be.

He smiles when he's happy and squeals when he plays.
We all show our happiness in much the same way.
We may not understand the reason for all the things he may do.
But don't taunt and tease others because they are not like you.

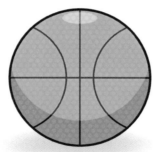

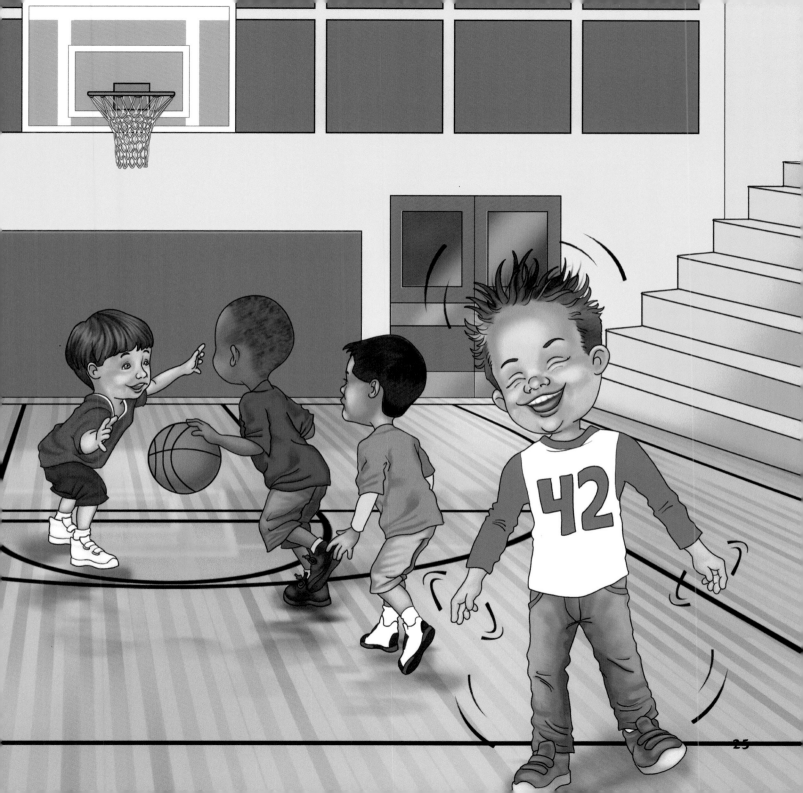

THEATER

now showing

It's Only Fair

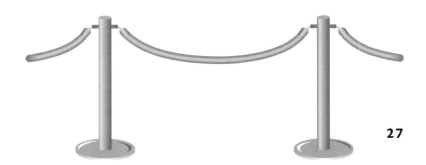

Now meet Blair, and before you stare,
let's hear his story; it's only fair.
You see, Blair has a set of helpers he uses at his side.
They are there to help him and support every stride.

He likes going to the movies, hanging out with friends,
and playing video games up to each day's end.
Friends call him a true sport who never gives in.
Every challenge is a game he's determined to win.

When you see him walking in public places,
don't stare or point or make strange faces.
Just be kind, for goodness sake.
It's always, by far, the right choice to make.

28

Unique Like You

Kacie is visually impaired, so she cannot see.
But she's a kid with talent; she learned the piano at three.
She reads with her fingertips things printed in Braille.
She walks with a guide stick when out on a trail.

Imagine what it would be like if it were you.
Before you judge others, put yourself in their shoes.
Cover both your eyes as you watch TV.
Try walking and playing – how hard would it be?

Even though Kacie is blind,
she's quite clever and kind.
Don't underestimate what others can do.
Kacie is unique, just like you.

Wherever You Go

Thank you for taking the time to read and see
and learn what it's like for kids with disabilities.
No doubt, there are others that you will see,
kids of all ages who have differences and disabilities.

Wherever you go, whatever you do.
Always treat others, as you want them to treat you.
You may want to tell others what you've learned today.
Share it in school, at home and at play.

Guide for Discussion

Don't Call Me Names is designed to help children understand other children who are in some way different. It teaches children to appreciate these differences and treat others as they want to be treated.

Its purpose is to promote respect, compassion, and friendship. Parents have the greatest influence in molding their children to become respectful and compassionate individuals. Teachers also play an important role. Use this book as a tool to open discussions with your child or children about the important lessons in each story.

- Respect one another's differences (we are all special and different from one another).

- Be thoughtful about what you do each and every day.

- Don't taunt and tease others because they are not like you.

- Don't stare or point or make strange faces (never make fun of people who are different from you in any way). Just be kind.

- Before you judge others, put yourself in their shoes.

- Don't underestimate what others can do.

- Always treat others, as you want them to treat you.

Model Questions

1. Do you know anyone who has a disability?

2. Can you name the kinds of helpers people with disabilities use to hear, walk, or see?

3. *Missy is much shorter than average ten-year-olds. She doesn't like it when people call her names.* How would you feel if you were called names or teased? How does it make you feel when others say nice things about you?

4. *Blair likes going to the movies, hanging out with friends, and playing video games.* What do you like to do in your spare time?

5. *Even though Kacie is blind, she's kind, smart, and talented. She started playing the piano when she was three-years-old.* What special talents do you have and what subject are you really good at in school?

6. After reading this book, what have you learned about kids with disabilities?

You may want to share what you've learned with family and friends.

Resources

www.allkidscan.com
www.jaylenschalllenge.org
www.kotb.com
www.pbskids.org/arthur/print/braille

Glossary

Autism   a developmental disability that causes the brain to work differently

Braille   letters and numbers printed as raised dots and read with the fingertips

Challenge   a difficult task, test of one's ability, a struggle

Compassion   caring about another person's feelings and well-being

Condition   a medical problem

Disability   lack of physical or mental ability to function normally

Hearing Impaired	hard of hearing, severely reduced hearing, deaf
Muscular Dystrophy	a genetic disorder that gradually weakens the body muscles
Respect	to show consideration for others, courteous behavior
Sign Language	a language that uses hand movements to communicate
Tracheostomy	a breathing tube a doctor inserts in the airway to help air reach the lungs
Visually Impaired	severely reduced vision, blind